**Disney**

# THE JUNGLE BOOK

# Adventure Story

# PaRRagon

Bath · New York · Singapore · Hong Kong · Cologne · Delhi
Melbourne · Amsterdam · Johannesburg · Auckland · Shenzhen

First published by Parragon in 2011
Parragon
Queen Street House
4 Queen Street
Bath BA1 1HE, UK

Printed in China

This is the story of The Jungle Book and the little Man-cub called Mowgli. Growing up in the jungle can be hard and there are many dangers lurking among the trees. But Mowgli has many friends and together they have lots of fun!
Now turn the page and begin Mowgli's adventure!

It was many years ago when I, Bagheera the panther, found a little lost Man-cub. He was alone and unprotected in the jungle of India. So I took the small boy to a nearby family of wolves I knew. As I had hoped, the mother wolf felt sorry for the Man-cub and she said to me, "Bagheera, leave him with us and we will raise him."

That is how little Mowgli, the Man-cub, came
to be brought up by jungle animals. He was
a favourite with all the wolf cubs of the pack.
They treated him just like a brother wolf.

Mowgli even made friends with the elephants and often marched in their Elephant Patrol. He loved living in the jungle.

Although Mowgli did not know it, I would often watch him from a distance to make sure he was safe. You see, the jungle also holds many dangers.

There was the crafty Kaa, who smacked his forked tongue at the sight of a "DE-LI-CI-OUS" Man-cub. I shudder to think how that tricky snake almost hypnotized Mowgli right into his greedy coils. Luckily, Mowgli called for help and I arrived in time to save him.

But Mowgli's real enemy was the fierce tiger, Shere Khan. Shere Khan hated all men and had sworn to kill the Man-cub. The tiger did not want to take a chance that the boy would grow up and become another hunter with a gun.

It was then that I spoke with Rama, Mowgli's
wolf father. "I'm sorry, Rama, but even the whole
wolf pack could not protect Mowgli from Shere
Khan. Everyone is in danger as long as the
Man-cub remains here."

Rama had known this day would come, and he
sadly agreed to let me take Mowgli to the safety
of the Man village.

The problem now was convincing Mowgli. While we were on one of our many walks into the jungle, I told Mowgli the bad news. "Mowgli, today we are not going home. Shere Khan has returned to the jungle and has promised to kill you. I am taking you to a Man village where you belong."

"But I don't want to live in the Man village. Besides, I can look after myself."

"Ha! You're so small! You would not last one day alone."

"Well, I'm not going!" And Mowgli stormed off deep into the jungle.

I knew the Man-cub would have to learn about the ways of the jungle for himself, so I let him go. But I followed close behind to see that he stayed out of trouble.

Unfortunately, who should the Man-cub meet first but that happy-go-lucky jungle bear, Baloo. Mowgli listened eagerly as Baloo sang to him about the simple, carefree life of a bear.

I had to step in. "Baloo," I explained, "Mowgli has to go back to the Man village."

"But they'll ruin him! They'll make a Man out of him."

Our discussion was cut short when a band of monkeys grabbed Mowgli and whisked him up into the tree tops.

"Come on, Baloo. They must be taking him to the ancient temple. That crazy monkey, King Louie, is behind this."

Soon Mowgli was face to face with King Louie. "Why have you brought me here?"

"Relax, Man-cub," said Louie. "We can help each other. I'll fix it so you can stay in the jungle, if you teach me the secret of Man's fire."

"But I don't know how to make a fire."

"Don't try to kid me, Man-cub! Tell me about Man's fire, so I can be like you."

It looked like Baloo and I had arrived just in time.

"Baloo," I said quietly, "you've got to create a disturbance so I can get Mowgli out of there."

Baloo took some leaves and a coconut shell and disguised himself as a monkey. Then he sang and danced with King Louie, while I found Mowgli.

But the disguise didn't fool Louie for long. "It's Baloo! Get that bear!"

In the wild chase that followed, Baloo bumped into a shaky old stone pillar and the ancient temple walls came crashing down around the monkeys. That gave us a chance to escape.

Now Baloo agreed with me that Mowgli must go back to the Man village. But Mowgli still couldn't understand.

"But Baloo – I want to stay here and be like you. You said we were partners. But you're just like old Bagheera. Neither of you likes me."

"Now hold on, Little Britches," said Baloo. "Bagheera and I are only trying to do what's best for you. You're a human and you belong with other humans."

Mowgli shook his head, turned and sadly walked away. This was the opportunity Shere Khan had been waiting for.

The tiger, who must have been following us for some time, saw the Man-cub alone and leaped out at Mowgli.

But the mighty Shere Khan fell with a thud a few inches away from the boy. Baloo had grabbed Shere Khan's tail at the last moment.

"Run, Mowgli!" shouted Baloo.

Shere Khan roared fiercely and lashed about, trying to get at Baloo. As long as the bear hung on tightly to Shere Khan's tail, he was safe from the tiger's razor-sharp teeth. But then Shere Khan cracked his big tail like a mighty whip and whirled Baloo to the ground.

Suddenly, a storm came up. A lightning bolt
flashed to earth and set a nearby tree alight.
Mowgli saw a way to save Baloo – the one thing
Shere Khan feared was fire.

Mowgli took a burning branch in his hand and ran toward the tiger. The fire frightened Shere Khan so much that he ran off like a scared kitten.

Baloo sighed in relief. "Nice work, Mowgli. We'll never see him around these parts again."

Mowgli was still convinced that he would never leave the jungle for any reason. But just then, he saw something he had never seen before. It was a girl. She was getting water at a pool, just outside the Man village.

Mowgli was enchanted. He had never seen another human before. "I want to get a closer look."

Mowgli crept closer to the girl until she could see him, too. She dropped her water jug and Mowgli stepped in to help her carry it back to her village.

I was pleased with the way things had turned out. "Ah, it had to happen, Baloo. Mowgli is where he belongs now."

"Yeah, I guess you're right. Well, come on, Baggie, buddy. Let's get back to where we belong." And home we went!